Welcome to Planet Reader!

Invite your child on a journey to a wonderful, imaginative place—
the limitless universe of reading! And there's no better traveling
companion than you, the parent. Every time you and your child read
together you send out an important message: Reading can be rewarding
and *fun*. This understanding is essential to helping your child build the
skills and confidence he or she needs as an emerging reader.

Here are some tips for sharing Planet Reader stories with your child:

Be open! Some children like to listen to or read the whole story and
then ask questions. Some children will stop on every page with a
question or a comment. Either way is fine; the most important thing
is that your child feels reading is a pleasurable experience.

Be understanding! Sometimes your child might need a direct answer.
If he or she points to a word and asks you to tell what it is, do so.
Other times, your child may want to sound out a word or stop to figure
out a sentence independently. Allow for both approaches.

Enjoy! The story and characters in this book were created especially for
your child's age group. Talk about the story. Take turns reading favorite
parts. Look at how the illustrations support the story and enhance the
reading experience.

And most of all, enjoy your child's journey into literacy. It's one of the
most important trips the two of you will ever take!

*For Christian, Callie, Luke, and
Miranda Jensen, whose mother works hard!*

This edition published in 2002.

Copyright © 1997 by Susan Schade and Jon Buller.

Published by Troll Communications L.L.C.

Planet Reader is a trademark of Troll Communications L.L.C.

Printed in the United States of America.   ISBN 0-8167-4374-6

10   9   8

PIG AT WORK

Susan Schade
& Jon Buller

I go to work
from eight to four.

It's just five minutes,

door . . .

to . . .

door!

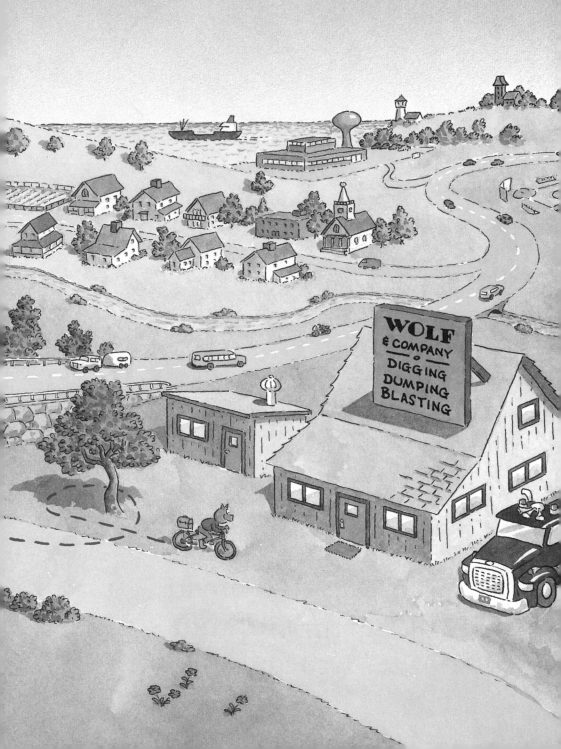

I bring an apple,
cheese, and bread.
I wear a hard hat
on my head.

Here's my boss.
His truck is big.

"Good morning, Wolf."
"Good morning, Pig."

We put the backhoe
on the truck.
We make wide turns.

We don't get stuck.

I get inside,
unload the rig.

I take control.
I'm Backhoe Pig!

I scrape a path
with one big sweep.

I dig a trench
that's three feet deep.

I back it up.
Beep-beep, beep-beep.

I dump the gravel
in a heap.

My good friends
the alligators
love their orange
excavators.

We move the earth.

We dig.

We dump.

We carry rocks.

We bury stumps.

We leave the biggest
rock for last.

Too big to move—
we'll have to. . .

We work all week.
We truck in fill.

We make a pond.
We make a hill.

The pond is full.
Our work is done.

We all jump in.
This job is fun!